The Cure for Consciousness

A Flash Novel

Peter Jelen

BareBackPress

BareBackPress
Hamilton, Ontario, Canada
For enquiries visit www.barebackpress.com
For information contact barebackpress@gmail.com
Cover layout and art: © P.Jelen

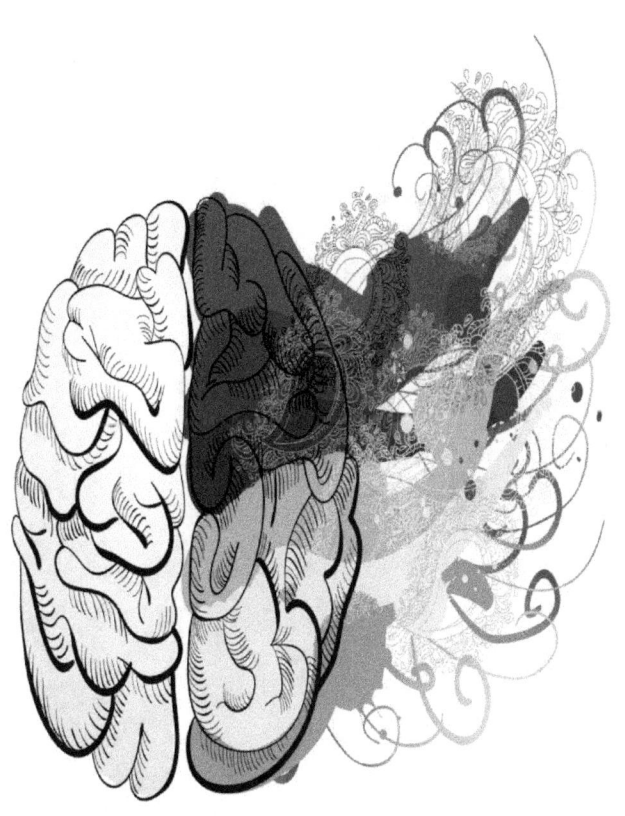

The Cure for Consciousness

A Flash Novel

Dear Reader,

This collection of anecdotes/recollections/musings/fantasies is written by my father, Ernie Lobe. It is being published against his wishes.

Before you begin, let me just say that I never knew how unhappy my father was. In fact, I didn't have the slightest inclination of his discontent. Although in my defense, he never showed it.

When I came across these writings I was awestruck. Not only because I was unable to believe how well he could hide his inner feelings, but more so because I was crushed by them. These journals changed my entire perception of him, and I truly, truly wish I'd never found them.

There are things in this volume in particular that leave me unsure. I do not know if my father was imagining, exaggerating, or if he really did do some of the things he claims he did. However, there are things he's written about that I can assure you did not happen. Or rather, did not happen the way he relates them. For instance, I did not stand up in the Olive Garden and announce that I'm "a cock chugging flamer. And proud of it!"

There are literally hundreds of these notebooks written by my father. However, this one, which you are about to read, is perhaps the most important. Not only because it shows the remarkable grand culmination of his life, but also because it truly illustrates the polarity of his nature.

With a Heavy and Remorseful Heart,
Charles Lobe

P.S. I would like to thank Peter Jelen and BareBackPress for publishing my father's story.

PROPERTY OF ERNIE LOBE

Day 19, 683

I have two options.
    Murder or suicide

Day 19, 684

Murder.
   I've chosen murder.

Plan to kill the Death Angel.

When she comes home from the store I'll be hiding on the roof of our shitty little house pretending to be adjusting the satellite dish.

When she's fumbling with her keys, just about to step onto the porch, I'll whistle ~ whistle with two fingers, really fuckin' loud, like a freight train pulling out of the station ~ stopping her in her slimy tracks.

When she looks up to find the source of this inhuman sound, she'll see me, perched on the roof with a cemented gargoyle smile curling my deranged face.

When she sees my smile, she'll see a big gray freak accident barreling through the sun spotted air onto her.

Then she'll see oblivion. Death. Darkness. And hopefully, if there is an eternity, if there is any justice in this vacuous, numb universe she will see my smile. And it will stay embedded/tattooed in her consciousness replaying, flickering, flapping, looping over and over and over again like a film reel containing only one image.

This image:

forever and ever and ever and ever and ever and ever and ever
and ever and ever and ever and ever and ever and ever and
ever and ever and ever and ever and ever and ever and ever
and ever and ever and ever and ever and ever and ever and
ever and ever and ever and ever and ever and ever and ever
and ever and ever and ever and ever and ever and ever and
ever and ever and ever and ever and ever and ever and ever
and ever and ever and ever and ever and ever and ever and
ever and ever and ever and ever and ever and ever and ever
and ever and ever and ever and ever and ever and ever and
ever and ever and ever and ever and ever and ever and ever
and ever and ever and ever and ever and ever and ever and
ever and ever and ever and ever and ever and ever and ever
and ever and ever and ever and ever and ever and ever and
ever and ever and ever and ever and ever and ever and ever
and ever and ever and ever and ever and ever and ever and
ever and ever and ever and ever and ever and ever and ever
and ever and ever and ever and ever and ever and ever and
ever and ever and ever and ever and ever and ever and ever
and ever and ever and ever and ever and ever and ever and
ever and ever and ever and ever and ever and ever and ever
and ever and ever and ever and ever and ever and ever and
ever and ever and ever and ever and ever and ever and ever
and ever and ever and ever and ever and ever and ever and
ever and ever and ever and ever and ever and ever and ever
and ever and ever and ever and ever and ever and ever and
ever and ever and ever and ever and ever and ever and ever
and ever and ever and ever and ever and ever and ever and
ever and ever and ever and ever and ever and ever and ever
and ever and ever and ever and ever and ever and ever and
ever and ever and ever and ever and ever and ever and ever
and ever and ever and ever and ever and ever and ever and
ever and ever and ever and ever and ever and ever and ever
and ever and ever and ever and ever and ever and ever and
ever and ever and ever and ever and ever and ever and ever
and ever and ever and ever and ever and ever and ever and
ever and ever and ever and ever and ever and ever and ever

and ever and ever and ever and ever and ever and ever and
ever and ever and ever and ever and ever and ever and ever
and ever and ever and ever and ever and ever and ever and
ever and ever and ever and ever and ever and ever and ever
and ever and ever and ever and ever and ever and ever and
ever and ever and ever and ever and ever and ever and ever
and ever and ever and ever and ever and ever and ever and
ever and ever and ever and ever and ever and ever and ever
and ever and ever and ever and ever and ever and ever and
ever and ever and ever and ever and ever and ever and ever
and ever and ever and ever and ever and ever and ever and
ever and ever and ever and ever and ever and ever and ever
and ever and ever and ever and ever and ever and ever and
ever and ever and ever and ever and ever and ever and ever
and ever and ever and ever and ever and ever and ever and
ever and ever and ever and ever and ever and ever and ever
and ever and ever and ever and ever and ever and ever and
ever and ever and ever and ever and ever and ever and ever
and ever and ever and ever and ever and ever and ever and
ever and ever and ever and ever and ever and ever and ever
and ever and ever and ever and ever and ever and ever and
ever and ever and ever and ever and ever and ever and ever
and ever and ever and ever and ever and ever and ever and
ever and ever and ever and ever and ever and ever and ever
and ever and ever and ever and ever and ever and ever and
ever and ever and ever and ever and ever and ever and ever
and ever and ever and ever and ever and ever and ever and
ever and ever and ever and ever and ever and ever and ever
and ever and ever and ever and ever and ever and ever and
ever and ever and ever and ever and ever and ever and ever
and ever and ever and ever and ever and ever and ever and
ever and ever and ever and ever and ever and ever and ever
and ever and ever and ever and ever and ever and ever and
ever and ever and ever and ever and ever and ever and ever
and ever and ever and ever and ever and ever and ever and
ever and ever and ever and ever and ever and ever and ever
and ever and ever and ever and ever and ever ~ forever

Wrong number.

Tried to call my insurance company today to update my policy and got the wrong number. Some woman answered.

Please, don't hang up!

Okay.

What's your name?

Ernie.

Hi Ernie. I'm Vivian.

Hi Vivian.

Are you lonely, Ernie?

Yeah, sometimes.

I'm lonely, Ernie. Very lonely.

Get a pet.

I'm a vegetarian.

So?

So I don't believe in keeping animals captive.

I thought vegetarians were only against eating meat.

Keeping them as prisoners is the same as eating them.

How is that?

I'd be consuming their freedom for my pleasure.

So why not just eat them for your pleasure?

Exactly, Ernie. Once their life becomes my responsibility it's all on me. What if I step on it? Or smother it to death during one of my fits. What if I forget to feed it?

Don't forget to feed it.

Even still, their happiness depends on me. And since animals don't talk. I won't know if I'm making it happy. I won't know if I'm being an animal abuser. I don't want to be an animal abuser, Ernie.

Well, how about a computer. Get a computer. I've heard people make a lot of friends on their computers.

I'm going bald, Ernie. I'm a woman and I'm going bald. Do you know what that's like?

No.
It's very stressful. Every time I look in the mirror and see more of my scalp the more stressed I get. And the more stressed I get the more hair I lose.
So don't look in the mirror.
Don't look in the mirror?
Yeah, or get a wig. A lot of women wear wigs. I heard Marilyn Monroe wore a wig.
Really?
Maybe.
Thanks Ernie.
For what.
For calling.
It wasn't on purpose.
That doesn't matter.
No, I guess it doesn't.
Who were you trying to call?
My insurance company.
What kind of insurance?
Life insurance.
I don't have life insurance. Or any kind of insurance.
So much the better.
Are you dying, Ernie?
Yes.
Is it cancer?
No.
Do you mind telling me what's wrong?
Life.
Life.
Yeah, life. I have a terminal case of consciousness.
We all do.
Yeah, but mine's really serious.
God once told me not to take life too serious.
God sounds pretty smart.
He is, Ernie. He's really smart. Do you want to meet him? I can introduce you.
Naw, that's okay. I don't need any more friends.

What about me, do you want to be my friend?

I don't like letting people down. And I don't think I'm going to be around much longer.

Are you moving?

You could say that.

Where are you moving to?

I'm not sure. Ask your friend God, maybe he'll know.

Yeah, he probably will.

So…

You want to stop talking, don't you?

It's not that I want to, it's just that I have to call my insurance company.

Life insurance.

Yeah.

Okay. Bye Ernie.

Bye.

Day 19, 691

Freaked out in the grocery store again today.
    This time at Wal-Mart.
    I'm wandering through the aisles for hours

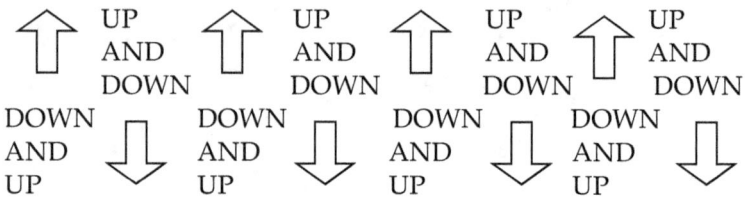

    trying to find the regular/normal square kind of crackers with salt on them.
    After three hours I finally find an employee. A young jizz filled condom with a ring in his nose. He's sitting on the lip of the dairy-cooler fiddling with his cell phone. I ask him where I can find regular/normal crackers with salt on them.
    I'm in the middle of something.
    What?
    Look, I'm busy. Dry goods ain't my section. Ask Topher.
    Where can I find Topher?
    The same place you can find the crackers.
    For another hour I wander

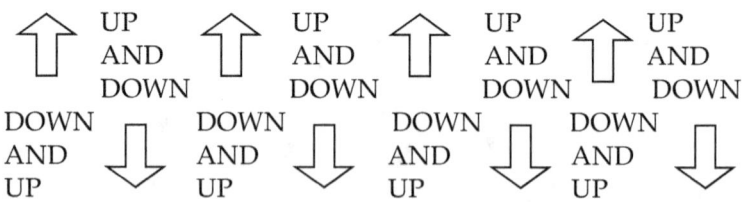

    looking for Topher.

I'm on the verge of tears, babbling to myself that I just want to find some crackers. Some regular/normal crackers. I just want to find Topher. Instead I find every other kind of cracker imaginable. Herb and garlic. Onion and chive. Low salt. No salt. Low carb. No carb. Fat free. Onion and garlic fat free. Multigrain. No carb multigrain. Animal shaped multigrain...

Now, I just want to leave in order to avoid another episode.

But now, I'm trapped.

Stuck in this maze of merchandise.

With shelves shifting and waving like an ocean of molten wax trying to swallow me up.

The products have come alive and started to taunt me. Slogans and slurs are being hurled by Captain Crunch and the Trix rabbit. The mouths of milk cartons rip open like talking vaginas and instruct me to destroy, break, ruin.

I cover my ears and fall to my knees.

I can't fight anymore.

I must obey.

They tell me that I must obey.

I crawl into the dairy section. Pull myself up to the edge of the egg cooler and begin pounding on the chickens that never were.

I pound and pound and pound. I pulverize a hundred thousand eggs with the jizz filled condom standing ten yards away still dicking around on his cell phone ~ never, even, noticing...ME

Day 19, 693

Came home.

Like usual, our shitty little house was a big crappy mess. The Death Angel was reclined on the grubby couch with her bloated varicose vein feet propped up on the vacuum cleaner. She blobbed there wearing only her filthy bra and torn up boxers with piss-stains at the apex of her vagina, Oreo cookie crumbs entrenched in the folds of her scaly flab.

Hey, hon. Tarkington give you any guff today?

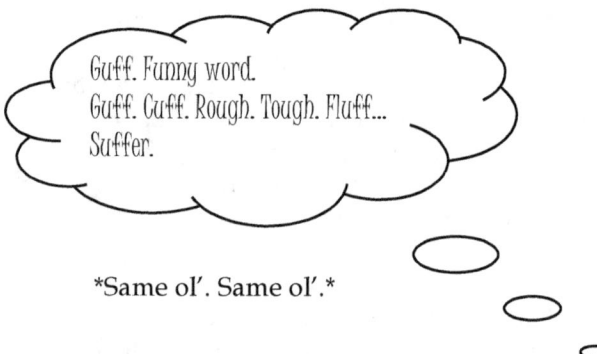

Guff. Funny word.
Guff. Cuff. Rough. Tough. Fluff...
Suffer.

Same ol'. Same ol'.

Later:
Before bed:

I force out a shit. Flush. Then clean the toilet bowl with her toothbrush.

Birthday.

The leeches got me an iPod for my birthday. They've taught me how to use it a dozen times, but I still can't figure the thing out. It was one of those gifts you buy for someone that's not really for them. I think they knew I would never learn how to use it and would give up. Then one of them would appropriate it. Either that, or they were embarrassed seeing their old man hobble to the bus stop every morning with a Walkman clipped to his hip.

No one uses a Walkman anymore, Dad.

I use a Walkman.

No offense. But you look crazy using a Walkman. It's like walking around with a beeper clipped to your belt instead of a cell phone.

Plus it can hold up to 4000 songs.

I don't even know 4000 songs. I can't even think of 4000 songs I'd ever want to listen to. My Walkman held a Sinatra tape. One Sinatra tape. My Walkman worked.

Now I have to walk to the bus stop every morning with these mushy seagull shit colored plugs in my ears pretending I know how to use it.

Now I have to walk to the bus stop without Frank drowning out the sounds of traffic and the whines of human misery hissing by me.

Now I have to pretend I know how to use this shitPod till the day I die just so I don't look…inept.

Day 19, 700

Antibiotics.
    Sometimes I eat old antibiotics I find in the medicine cabinet even when I'm not sick.
    I like knowing that they'll kill the bacteria in my body.
    I think some part of me thinks that I have bacteria in my brain. Really dangerous bacteria. And if I eat these old antibiotics I'll miraculously be cured.

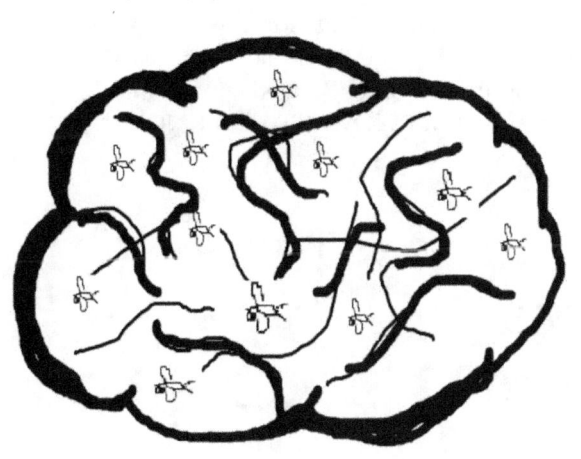

Day 19, 710

When my alarm clock squeals at 5:45 AM the Death Angel rolls over and cheerfully whispers in my ear *Hon, it's time to get up for work.*

When my alarm clock tears me out of my slumber and the Death Angel rolls over to me and cheerfully says *Hon, it's time to get up for work* I envision myself ripping the plug out of the wall, wrapping the black electrical cord around my fist and smashing her big bucked-teeth down into her pasty pink mouth, screaming, *I KNOW BITCH! I KNOW!*

I tell her I'm having a bad day.

Like I feel like cutting my wrists to let the pain bleed out.

She goes on reading the newspaper.

I sink into a warm bath and stare at her Gillette resting in the soap dish contemplating suicide for an hour.

But I don't do it.

Only because I know that it would make her…happy.

Day 19, 715

Lamictal.
    Been eating a few of her Lamictal every day for the past month. Thought maybe I'm fucked up like she is. Thought it might help.
    It didn't.
    It just made her more crazy because she ran out of pills and was too manic to go the doctor to get a renewal on the prescription.

Day 19, 717

The nursing home.

She came home from the nursing home clicking her heels together and whistling that song about the witch being dead from the Wizard of Oz.

Don't you wanna know why I'm so happy?

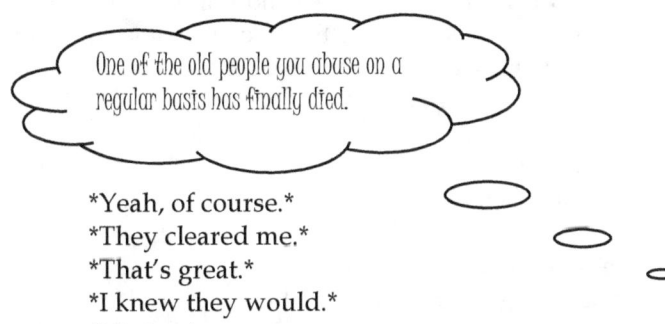

One of the old people you abuse on a regular basis has finally died.

Yeah, of course.
They cleared me.
That's great.
I knew they would.
Me too.

Everyone knows I wouldn't hurt a fly. Seriously, even when I see a spider in the house, you know what I'm like. I always cover it up with a glass, slip a sheet of paper under it and let it go outside. Have you ever seen me ever hurt anything?

No, Angel. Never.

I don't blame them though. She did have bruises. They needed to look into it. I would want an investigation too if that happened to my mother.

Of course.

It was probably one of those Filipinos. They're awful. Everyone knows Filipinos mistreat the elderly. They don't have the same value for human life over there. Then they come to our country and think they can do the same.

Keep your eyes peeled.

I will. Believe me I will. How was your day? Did Tarkington give you any guff?

Plan to murder Tarkington.

I'm hiding behind the door in the stockroom with the lights off.

I don't care if I get caught.

I'm hiding in the stockroom waiting for him with one hand full of muffin batter, the other hand full of cookie dough.

When he comes through the door I spring out at him growling and foaming like a movie zombie.

What the fuck, Lobe?

Head butt.

Testicle kick.

He's on his knees.

I'm shoving cookie dough into his throat.

He's on his back.

I'm stuffing muffin batter up his nose.

His eyes are rolling back.

His breathing is labored.

He's looking up at me like, *What the fuck, Lobe?*

I'm looking down on him like, *I just found the cure for consciousness.*

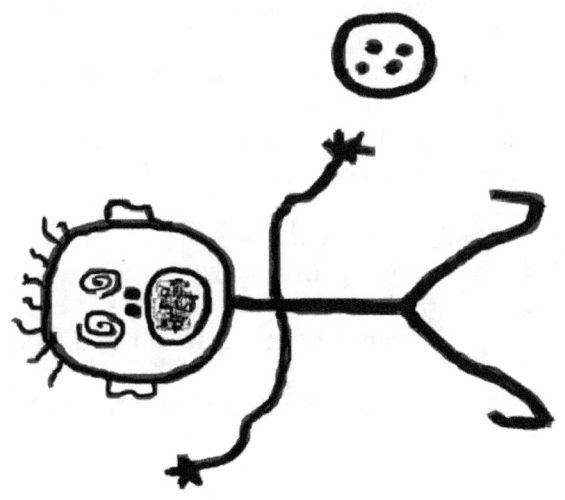

Gluten.

Everyone's talking about gluten.

Every day when I'm at work, some stinky rotten cock or some sour carnivorous vagina will ask me if the muffins have gluten in them. Five years ago they were asking about trans-fat. Ten years ago they were asking about MSG. Twenty years ago no one gave a shit what was in their food. They just ate it, and enjoyed eating it.

Now, when I'm asked this question about gluten, I pretend to call Tarkington.

I pretend I don't know the answer.

Gluten? How do you spell that?

G.L.U.T.E.N.?

Hum, never heard of it.

You don't know about gluten?

No, I'm sorry I don't, ma'am.

Well, is there anyone here that knows if the muffins have gluten?

I can ask the owner, Mr. Tarkington for you?

Could you?

Sure, yeah. No problem. He's out at the moment, but if you wait a minute I'll call him up.

Thanks.

What did you say that stuff was?

Gluten.

Gluten. Got it./Hello, Mr. Tarkington. Yeah, I have a customer here that would like to know if the muffins have gluten in them. I'm not sure, sir. Hold on./Excuse me, ma'am. Mr. Tarkington wants to know what gluten is.

It's like, stuff they put in food.

Yes, but…what is it? Is it poisonous or something?

No, it's not poisonous. It's like…I don't know how to explain it.

Sir, yes, she says she doesn't know how to explain it./ Ma'am, he says he thinks they probably don't, but he's not sure. They definitely don't have MSG or trans fat.
Probably, or don't have gluten?
Probably don't.
This is ridiculous.
I could pretend to call the manufacturer if you want?
Would you?
Sure, no problem.

Day 19, 730

Chewing tobacco.

No one chews tobacco anymore. I'm lucky there's still one store in this wasteland that sells my peppermint Skoal. It's next to the liquor store in the Cherry Housing Projects. The shop's run by a 67 year old black man named Clarence who's always bragging to me that he's never been robbed.

Pharmacy been robbed. Used car lot across the street been robbed. Liquor store been robbed plenty a times. Me. I never been robbed.

I've never been robbed either.

Damned fools even robbed the post office. Can you believe it?

Unbelievable.

Believe it.

Coming out party.

Last night the leeches told us they wanted to take us out to dinner at the Olive Garden for a little get together with all of their friends. I assumed this dinner was a thank you from the boy leech since he's finally gotten a job as a bartender at some bar. They didn't tell me or the Death Angel exactly why they were taking us out until midway through my Bolognaise, until both of the leeches were slurring drunk and their friends were drum/clinking their glasses with the cutlery egging them on to do it.

Do what?

Alright, alright, alright! Mom, Dad, you guys may or may not have already figured this out, but... I'm gay! I'm a fag. A cock chugging flamer. And proud of it!

Now it was the girl leech's turn. She stood up, made a peace symbol with her fingers, reversed it, put the fingers up to her lips and flicked her tongue like a snake miming cunnilingus.

And I'm a finger lickin' good, dildo ramming dyke!

Everyone in the restaurant heard this.

Everyone in the restaurant applauded this.

Complete strangers were overjoyed and teary eyed ~ reacting as if they'd just witnessed a good old-fashioned one-kneed proposal.

The lines must have gotten crossed when we sharing your womb, Mom. Ha, ha, ha.

Everyone laughed. But the audience was waiting for my reaction with bated breath.

Would I accept them? Would I reject them?

I got up.

Gave the cock-sucking leech a kiss on the cheek, told him that I'd love him no matter what.

Then I hugged the muff munching leech. Told her the same thing.

The entire Olive Garden came to a halt. Condoms, tampons, and enemas were out of their seats and cheering for the happy ending, shouting bravo, bravo, like the curtain had just came down at the end of a Broadway hit on opening night.

Day 19, 735

This murder.

      This murder of mine's been a long time coming. Perhaps it was inevitable. If God makes people gay ~ if it's not a choice, God must've made me this way too.

Day 19, 738

Tarkington asks me if I've ever heard of this gluten stuff.
  No sir, can't say that I have.
  Well, apparently a lot of people don't want it in their food anymore.
  Is it poisonous?
  No. They just don't like it. Anyway, we're gonna start baking gluten free stuff.
  How will we do that?
  We're gonna bake without gluten?
  I understand, but how will we take out the gluten?
  We won't. The manufacturer will.
  Sir, what exactly is gluten?
  It has something to do with food production and modification.
  Oh, so it's something they add to the food. Like MSG.
  How the fuck should I know, Lobe? I ain't no scientist. Now go whip up a batch of onion bagel dough.

Onion bagels.
Some days I'll cut myself, wrap the wound in gauze. After a couple of days when the gauze is all caked with tacky yellow pus I'll chop it up as fine as ground black pepper and sprinkle it into the onion bagel dough.

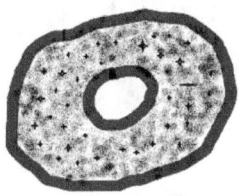

Cranberry muffins.
Sometimes when I cut myself I'll collect the blood in a big bowl and add flour and eggs to it and cook it in the microwave on high heat for five minutes until it gets all coagulated and sticky. Then I'll make little blood balls that look like cranberries and add them to the cranberry muffins before pushing them into the oven.

Chocolate chip cookies.
Sometimes I'll scoop nibblets of my antibiotic shit out of the toilet and sprinkle it into the chocolate chip cookie mix.

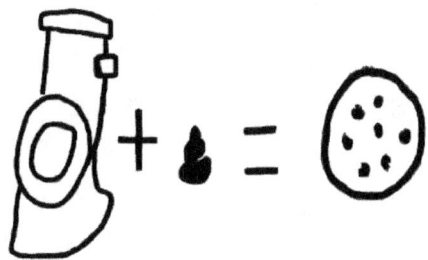

Onion bagels. Cranberry muffins. Chocolate chip cookies. Those are our most popular sellers. I think it's because people unconsciously enjoy eating human waste-products. They have a primeval urge to devour each other. That's why a baby's first instinct is to suck its mother's breast. That's why men and women derive pleasure from sucking on each other's genitals and kissing each other on the mouth.

People are cannibals.

They just don't act on it.

The cock eating, jizz drinking leech calls me at work.
  I don't recognize his voice. It's different than before.
It's changed. His voice is higher. He has a lisp. He sounds like
the labia lapping lesbian leech.
  You busy, Dad?
  Never too busy for you, son. What's up?
  *Just wondering if you're still using that iPod me and
Connie got you?*
  Yeah, of course. Every day.
  Oh.
  Why?
  *I was hoping I could borrow it this weekend. Paul's
taking me to Blue Mountain.*
  Yeah, sure. Swing by and pick it up.
  Great. Thanks. I'll be by around noon.
  *I'll whip up a batch of chocolate chip cookies for you
guys to take with you.*
  That'd be great, Dad.

Day 19, 749

Finally got a hold of my insurance company. They said that in order to get a million dollar policy I'd have to get a physical. Make sure that I don't have any terminal diseases like AIDS or cancer or Hodgkin's Lymphoma. They didn't say anything about consciousness.

Clarence, the old black man who's always bragging about never getting robbed, still hasn't gotten robbed. But the liquor store across the street got robbed again.

Saw the whole thing happen. Guys came in with shotguns and ski masks, started shooting up the place. Blew the owner's head off. The damned rice-eater never had a chance.

They catch them?

Naw, they never catch'em.

You tell the police what you saw?

I don't wanna end up like that chink. Think the only reason I never been robbed or fucked with all these years is because I keep my eyes closed, if you know what I mean.

Yeah, I know what you mean.

Plan to rob and maybe murder Clarence.

When he SEES me coming, he'll smile affably thinking he's going make a dime from the cancer he's giving my mouth.

He won't SEE the two nickel plated 45's stuffed in the holsters under my armpits.

When he SEES me coming, he'll turn around to grab my daily pack of chew.

He won't SEE me pulling out the two nickel plated 45's.

When he turns around he'll SEE that I'm shoving the barrels of the nickel plated 45's into his eyes.

When he's SEES, finally SEES this, I'll hop over the counter, throw him to the ground and step on his throat to muffle his pleas for help, push the barrels so deep into his sockets that his eyes will pop like balloons.

When he HEARS his eyes pop like balloons, I'll rob him. I'll steal one pack of chew. Then I'll spit a glob of tobacco into each of his mashed up eyes and tell him that he's a horrible citizen, a contagious blight in the community.

These cookies taste like shit.

Some used condom and his rotten tampon wife come into the bakery today with their soon to be soiled tampon daughter to complain about a batch of chocolate chips he bought earlier in the day.

These cookies taste like shit.

He slams the box onto the counter.

Really?

Eat one if you don't believe me.

Tarkington comes out of his office and asks me what the condom's problem is.

This gentleman thinks the cookies taste a little off.

No! They don't taste a little off. They taste like shit. And I don't mean metaphorically. I mean they taste like human shit.

How would you know what human shit tastes like? Have you eaten shit before?

Don't get lippy with me asshole, I don't give a fuck if you run this place, you fed my family shit. You're lucky I don't hop over this counter and throttle you.

First of all, shit isn't the secret ingredient in our cookies. Secondly, I'd like to see you try and get over this counter when I got a .38, and a license to carry a concealed weapon permit in my pocket.

Are you threatening me?

No, I'm promising you that if you come over this counter I'll consider it an attempt to rob my shop. And I'll blow a hole in you.

What the fuck kind of bakery is this?

The kind that doesn't take any guff.

Come on, Ron. This guy's a nut. Let's just go.

I'll be back, you fuck. This ain't over.

Yeah, yeah, yeah.

The used condom, the rotten tampon, and their soon to be soiled tampon daughter head for the door.

Tarkington dips his hand into the box left behind and shoves one of the shit cookies in his mouth.

Goddamn, these cookies really do taste like shit.

Day 19, 764

Consciousness didn't show up in the blood work. I don't have AIDS, or cancer, or Hodgkin's Lymphoma.
So now, it's whenever I'm ready.

The Filipinos.

Every other day, when my Death Angel comes back from the nursing home I have to hear about the Filipinos.

Every other day, when she slimes her way through the front door with crazy pinwheel spinning eyes I listen to her farting and belching about how Filipinos are the most disgusting example of human life on the entire planet. How they're worse than niggers and spics combined. How someone should drop a 10 000 ton nuclear bomb on Manila and wipe them out.

I listen to her racist, genocidal ideas intently. Find myself agreeing. Not because I agree, but because I don't want to argue.

Agree. Argue.

Argue. Agree.

She's a fruit loop, a total wack-a-doo. There's no point in arguing with a wack-a-doo.

There's no point in agreeing either.

It's just... easier.

Am I right, Ernie? Don't you agree?

Agree. I agree.

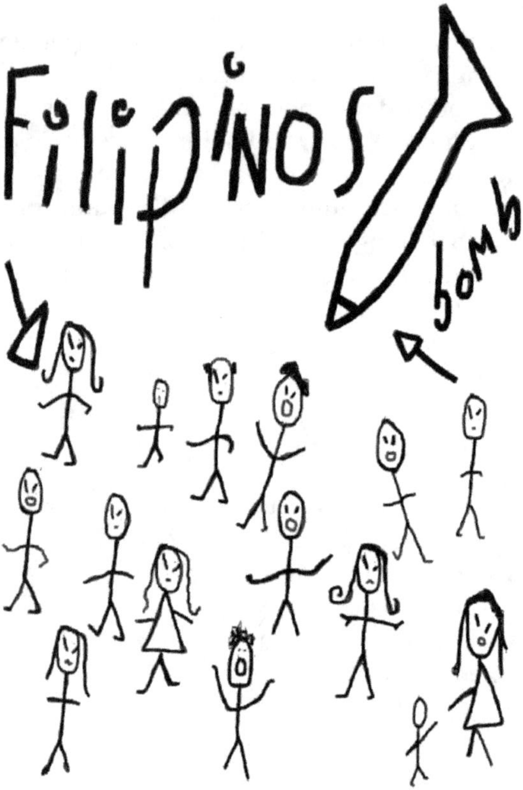
Filipinos
bomb

Day 19, 773

It happened again at Wal-Mart.

It happened when I finally found regular/normal crackers, the white square with salt on them kind

It happened when I was at the checkout loading everything onto the belt.

It happened when I saw that my crackers weren't actually the regular/normal kind.

It happened when I saw that someone or something in this oozing, puss exploding Gonorrhea universe was playing a horrible, cruel joke on me by making the regular/normal kind of crackers...**Now Gluten Free!**

I don't remember exactly what happened next.

I ██████ed out after that.

All I remember is that it took whatever will I have left in me not to end up on the 11 o'clock news tonight.

All I remember is that it took three stock boys and a dairy manager to cart me out of there.

All I remember is that I woke up in the parking lot hours later with foam caked around my lips and crusty yellow bile staining the front of my shirt.

Day 19, 777

My murder.
        I'm going to do my murder.
        Soon.

Been biting myself lately.

Been biting myself so hard lately that my forearms look like I've been attacked by a bear trap.

Usually, when I bite myself, I'm at work.

Usually, I'll spit the pieces into the banana muffin batter.

Usually, people don't notice that they're cannibals.

They don't care if the muffins are flesh free.

They only ask about gluten.

They only care about gluten.

Day 19, 784

The condom that ate the shit cookies came back to the bakery today with a couple of magnum condom buddies to beat the shit out of Tarkington, but Tarkington wasn't there.

I told the condom and his buddies he'll be back around five when my shift finishes.

The condom said thank you and asked me not to tell Tarkington that he came by.

You didn't see us.

I didn't SEE anything.

The Death Angel.

    She hasn't been taking her Lamictal.

    She's been feeling fine and doesn't need it.

    She's finding herself.

    She's finding out who's been abusing the elderly.

    She feels whole.

    She wants me to feel whole with her.

    She's going to have a break down after my murder.

    She's probably going to kill herself.

    I hope she doesn't. I really hope she doesn't.

    I hope the money will change her mind.

    I hope the money stops her from killing herself.

    I need this break. This alone time.

    That's the point of this murder.

Day 19, 788

Been staking out the Cherry Housing Projects looking for a good place to do my murder.

Based on what Clarence has told me and the recon I've done the best place to do my murder is in front of the liquor store.

The condoms.

The condoms got to Tarkington. They got to him really good according to Tarkington's tampon.

He was in the ICU last night, Ernie. His face is a mess.

That's awful. Will he be okay?

He'll pull through.

Do the police have any idea who did it?

Brian's been sedated. And his jaw is wired shut, so even when he wakes up it's not going to be easy for him to give the police much information. Did anything out of the ordinary happen at the shop in the last few days?

No, nothing.

He didn't have an argument with a customer or something?

Not as far as I know.

Did he mention anything, anything at all to you?

Not a word.

You know how Brian can overreact sometimes. I think something must've happened at the shop. Are you sure you didn't see something, Ernie?

I didn't SEE anything.

The police may come by to talk to you if that's alright.

Of course, no problem. I'll do whatever I can to help.

Thanks Ernie. You sure you'll be alright running things while he's gone.

Second nature.

Please, let me know if you need anything, anything at all. Okay Ernie?

Don't worry about me. You have more than enough to be concerned about. Please give my sympathy to kids. Brian's in my prayers. I'll come by the hospital tomorrow.

That'd be sweet of you.

I'll bring some cookies for everyone.

Chocolate chip?
Is there any other kind?

Gluten free mix.

The gluten free muffin mix arrives. It arrives at 5: 27 PM along with the gluten free cookie mix.

The expired prophylactic wheeling it in wants to know where to put it.

The stock room.

What are you gonna do with the old mix?

Use it.

But it's not gluten free.

People like to have... options.

But why would someone want muffins or cookies with gluten in them when they can have muffins or cookies without gluten?

Some people like gluten.

Who?

Me.

But that's like liking cholesterol, or trans fat, or MSG.

Really?

Yeah, really.

So I shouldn't like it anymore.

It's not a matter of liking it. Just avoiding it.

What...exactly...is gluten?

Do I look like a chemistry teacher? Alls I know is it ain't good for you.

Hey, I'm getting ready to close up, got a whole bunch of leftover cookies and muffins. Would you like to take them home to your family?

Do they have gluten?

Yes, but I'm sure a little gluten won't kill them.

Yeah, sure. Why not?

Do you like chocolate chip cookies?

Is there any other kind?

Day 19, 795

Stayed late last night testing out the new gluten free mixes.

Came up with a new recipe.

Tested one of the new recipes out on the leeches and the Death Angel.

What's in it? Peppermint? I taste peppermint.

Peppermint and something else...what are these little black shreds?

That's the peppermint.

You sure these are gluten free, Dad?

They're supposed to be.

Is everything going to be gluten free at the bakery now?

No, not everything.

It should be. Everyone's going gluten free. Me and Paul have been on a zero gluten diet for three weeks.

Ernie, these smell a little odd.

That's what gluten free is supposed to smell like, Mom.

I noticed the smell too when I prepared the dough. I think it's the new mix.

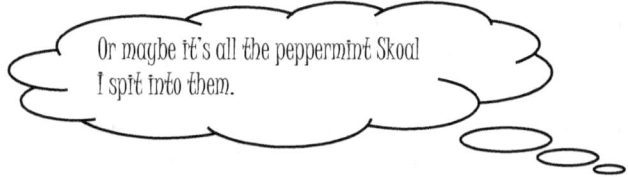

Or maybe it's all the peppermint Skoal I spit into them.

Dad, do these muffins have meat in them?

Of course not.

You sure, 'cause this one kind of tastes like pork.

It's has to be this new mix. I'd better tell Tarkington.

Day 19, 800

I want my murder to be done with a gun. I don't want it done slow and painful. Like life.

Day 19, 801

Offered up free samples of our new gluten free line to the tampons and condoms today.

No one complained about the baked goods containing human flesh, blood, feces, or chewing tobacco spit.

Usually tampons and condoms don't complain when you give them free stuff.

Neither do I.

The Death Angel whipped open the front door and chucked her purse across the living-room. I was sitting on the couch watching Hoarders and didn't notice she'd punched a hole in the wall until she came over to me and stood in front of the TV.

     Don't you wanna know what's wrong?

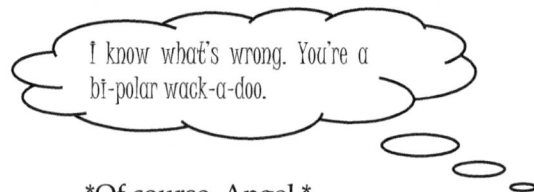

     Of course, Angel.
     So turn off the TV!
     I mute it.
     Turn it off, or I swear to God I'll smash it!
     Okay, Angel. Relax. Tell me what's wrong?
     The Filipinos! That's what's wrong!
     What happened?
     Mrs. Cornworth died!
     So?
     The police came. They think she was murdered! Smothered! Asphyxiated!
     By one of the Filipinos?
     No! By me!
     By you! But you'd never do something like that.
     That's what I told the detective.
     Do you think one of the Filipinos is trying to frame you?
     They all are. They're all trying to frame me.
     Did you tell the detective this?
     Duh! Yeah.
     How did they frame you?
     If I knew, I'd know.
     When did it happen, Angel?

While I was watching Mrs. Cornworth a Moses buzzed for help and when I went to check-up on him one of those fermenting Filipino cunts snuck into the room.
    Aren't there cameras?
    Not in the rooms, only in the hallways.
    So the detective will see one of them going into the room when he checks the cameras.
    She!
    She what?
    The detective is a she! And she already checked the cameras, and the Filipinos already tampered with the tapes. It only shows ME going into the room!
    That's a problem.
    Yeah, no shit it's a problem.
    So what're you going to do?
    Hire the best Jew in the city and fight!
    How come they didn't arrest you?
    They're building a case. They're not gonna jump the gun and have it thrown out in court.
    Maybe you should take your Lamictal.
    Take my fucking Lamictal!
    Or don't.
    You think taking my Lamictal is gonna stop the investigation!
    No, but it'll help you...deal...with it.
    Oh I'll deal with it. I'll fight this to the death. That's how I'll deal with it!
    You promise you won't do anything...silly.
    Like kill my fucking self?
    Yeah.
    I'll walk in there with a flamethrower and kill every one of those Filipino cunts before I kill MYself. They're the ones that deserve to die. Not me.
    I agree.

Day 19, 806

I believe her.

I believe she'll roast every last one of those fermenting Filipino cunts before she takes her own life.

Day 19, 808

This murder wrap stuff is a real blessing in disguise. I know now that when my murder happens the Death Angel will pretty much ignore it.

> Wait. Who am I kidding?
> She would've ignored it anyway.

B▦l∞ah farg™ ♫in mar♀gin shuk♂arkin⅞g smuc∩kia chsay,lofop.NΦaurΔdasξitrβlr♣ifohdyeswmds≡oawieψdpoЖ

   LdispaβwÉ

   Àiuff, anciç.

   Ko▦p fyléè. Yççm⁴¿.

   Baslпk.

   Ωmçà@l, aywows!

   =9#&(☼)≠

Regular/normal crackers.

I finally found the regular/normal crackers with salt on them kind at 7/Eleven today.

Elated. Ecstatic. In ecstasy, I hurried up to the festering semen filled condom at the counter.

They're not showing up.

What does that mean?

It means I don't know how much they cost.

Meaning?

Is English your second language, bro-jo. It means I don't know how much they cost.

I understand that. I mean, what do we do about it?

Nothing.

Nothing?

Yeah, nothing.

You can't sell them to me?

See this barcode scanner?

Yeah.

It's connected to this cash register. Following me so far? Good. Now, if this barcode scanner doesn't know the price, neither does the cash register, which MEANS, neither do I. Which MEANS, I can't sell them to you because I don't know how much they cost.

$2.39 plus tax.

*So *you* say.*

That's what they've been costing for the last three years.

How do I know that?

Okay, how much do you want for them?

Can't do it, bro-jo. Even if you give me fifty bucks I can't do it. There's no way of putting them in the system.

Are you telling me that you wouldn't sell these crackers for fifty dollars?

How do I know you ain't a secret shopper that's gonna rat me out to the boss. I'm not willing to lose my job just so you can get some stupid crackers.

Are you willing to stop me?

Stop you from what?

I slapped a five dollar bill on the counter, grabbed the crackers out of his hand and headed for the door.

Hey, you can't do that!

Try to stop me. I dare you.

Yeah right. You're a total psycho, bro-jo. Take your stupid crackers.

Thanks...bro-jo.

Day 19, 813

I come home and slither away. I go upstairs to our dirty/rotten/putrid/disgusting/wretched/vomit-inducing bedroom. I sit down here on the stool in front of the mirror where the Death Angel usually sits to put on her make-up, where she makes herself look like a human being, a being of humanity.

Staring at myself, at this thing, this creature, at this shell of a human being, I undress.

If the Giants lose tonight I'm going to do it tonight.

Do it for sure.

I open up the jewelry box.

I put on my wedding ring.

I slip the gold Bvlgari my father gave me around my wrist instead of cutting it.

I link my gold chain around my neck instead hanging myself with a belt.

I slither over to the closet, put on my suit. My gold cufflinks.

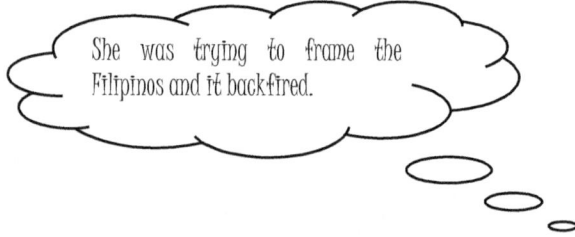

She was trying to frame the Filipinos and it backfired.

I look at myself ~ my desolate, rancorous, perverted, demented, loathsome self ~ one last time in the mirror.

I turn on the radio.

Tune into the Giants game.

It's down to the two minute warning.

The Giants are losing.

35 to 7.

On my way to the bus stop

I pray my murder is done with a gun. I don't
want it done slowly and painfully. Like life.

At the Cherry Housing Projects.
        I stand in front of the liquor store.
        Murder Central.
        I stand at Murder Central checking my watch.
        Opening my wallet.
        Eating my crackers.
        My last meal.
        I stand.
        I wait...
....
....
....
....
....
....
....
....
....
....
....
....
....
....
....
....
....

....
....
....continue to wait................
....
....
....
....
................still..waiting...
....
....
....
....
....
....
................................still there................................
....
....
....
....
....
....
................still waiting..
....
....
....
....
....
....
....now................
....
....
....
....
................................finally................................
....
....

...........................Three young men wearing red bandanas approach.

The young men wearing red bandanas are no more than 25 years old.

One of them has a tattoo on his neck.

He nudges the other two guys.
They stop and stare.
They check me out.
I prepare myself for my murder.
I hope they have guns.
I hope they shoot me until their clips are empty.
They start to come.
They stride menacingly.
They surround me.
You lost, partner?
I was.
No, I think you's lost.
I would know if I were lost. I'm not lost.
What time is it, dawg?
10:34.
Naw, dawg. It's time to gimmie yo watch.
I don't think so.
You don't think so?
No.
No?
You got shit in your ears. I said no.
You's a brave mutherfucka.
And you're a piece of shit spic.
You wants to get merked?
Merked. What does that mean? Is that nigger talk. I don't understand nigger.

They chuckle amusedly. Diablo smiles. But it's not a friendly smile. It's more of a devious, mischievous, I'm-going-to-kill-you smile.

He lifts up the front of his checkered shirt and reaches into his waistline. He's just about to pull out his gun and give me a lethal injection of lead when a black and white with its cherries on cruises up behind them splashing red and blue light across my face.

Two uniforms get out and approach, hands on their guns, asking if there's a problem.

No Officer Dan, no problem at all, right Whitey.

No problem until you interrupted us.

What're you doing here?

These nice gentlemen were giving me directions.

Directions, yeah. So you think we're stupid. We know what you're doing in this part of town. You're trying to score.

Score what?

Drugs.

I came here to get chewing tobacco. Ask Clarence over there, he's the only guy in town that still sells it.

Bullshit! You're a piece of shit junky.

I'm not a junky.

You think I don't know a piece of shit junky when I see one?

I'm not a junky.

Are you giving us guff? Maybe we should slap the cuffs on him.

You'd better get in your car and go home before we take you to OUR house.

I don't have a car.

That's because you're a piece of shit junky who spends all of his money on crack!

Looks like a tweaker to me, Dan.

What's a tweaker?

You're a tweaker.

Would love to go for Officer Dan's gun.

Would pay to get my brains blown out right here at Murder Central.

But the policy.

The policy is void if I get murdered while committing a felony.

So...

I don't go for his gun.

I let them finish doing their tough-guy cop bullshit and head back to my cage, to the Death Angel and the leeches. Eat a handful of antibiotics and brew up a big loose liquidy shit for tomorrow's batch of chocolate chips.

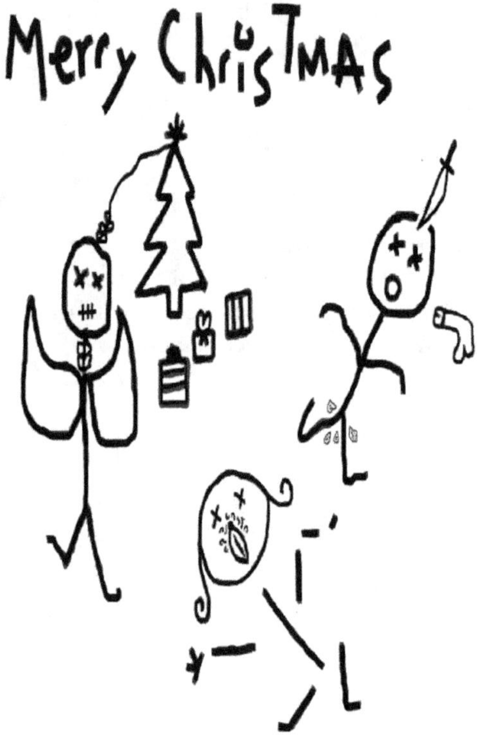
Merry ChrisTMAS

Christmas.

The leeches got me an iPhone for Christmas.

I got them an even bigger life insurance policy and $100 gift cards for Tower Records.

No one buys records anymore, Dad.

I know that. Tower Records sells CD's.

No one buys CD's either.

Really?

Yeah. Really. Only retards and old people still buy CD's. Everything's free on the Internet.

You could've at least gotten us iTunes gift cards.

Sorry guys. I feel bad.

That's okay. I'll sell it to a retard or something.

I love the iPhone though. This is amazing.

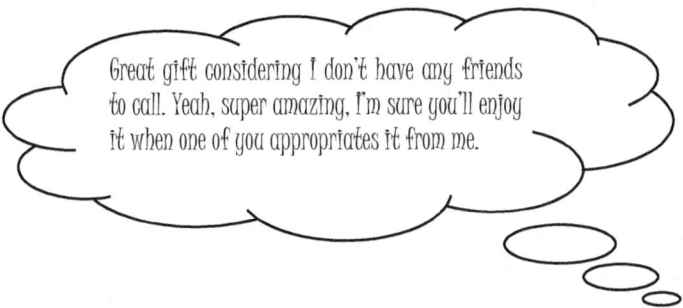

Great gift considering I don't have any friends to call. Yeah, super amazing, I'm sure you'll enjoy it when one of you appropriates it from me.

Really guys. Thanks so much. You didn't have to do this. Wow, its great.

It's got the Internet and tons of apps.

What's an app?

Application. These square things. You just touch it and it'll do stuff.

What kind of stuff?

*Here, I'll show you. See this app?"

Gaydar.

Yeah, all you gotta do is touch it and it'll give you a list of all the gay and lesbian clubs, bars, bistros, and restaurants within a 100 mile radius of where you are.

It's awesome, Dad. No matter where you are in the world you'll be able to find other gay joints.

But I'm not gay.

Yeah, but if you were...

This one's champ too, Dad.

Ohhhh, Robo-You. Aw yeah. Here, watch. I'm gonna take your picture and then upload it to Robo-You and its gonna show what you'd look like if you were a robot.

Done. Here. See. This is you as a robot.

Wow, that is...champ.

Check this one out, Knotical Mile. It shows you how to tie and untie all different kinds of knots.

Knots?

Yeah, it's like if you ever got tied up by a kidnapper you'd be able to get free.

Or if you sail.

I don't sail.

Or even if you throw a dinner party and wanna make neat napkin knots to impress your guests.

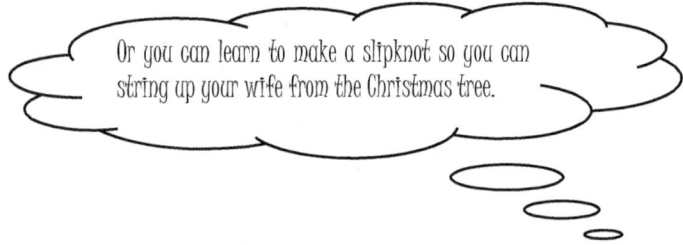

Or you can learn to make a slipknot so you can string up your wife from the Christmas tree.

Show him App-pedia.

Oh yeah. Here, look Dad. You'll probably like this one the best. It's an encyclopedia of all the apps. I'm practically addicted to App-pedia.

Is there anything on there that can tell me about gluten?

Oh for sure. All you gotta do is Google it.

How do I do that?

Just press this blue e here. Wait a sec. Okay, now you're on Google. So just type in whatever question you have.

Whatever question I have, and it'll tell me the answer?

Yeah.

So it's like…God.

Yeah, I guess. Kinda.

Here, try it.

So I type, on that little key pad, with my big fat fingers:

WHAT IS GLUTEN?

m/z 595.6 [M+H]

Day 19, 830

Tried to get murdered at the liquor store again today.
    Didn't happen.
    Four crackers left.
    Getting
    really,
    really,
    really,

frustrated

Day 19, 833

Asked Goddle where I can find a hit man to have myself murdered.

Goddle referred me to Craig.

Craig has a list with thousands of people selling, buying, and offering services.

I didn't find any hit men though. I only found condoms and tampons who were willing to piss in my mouth for money.

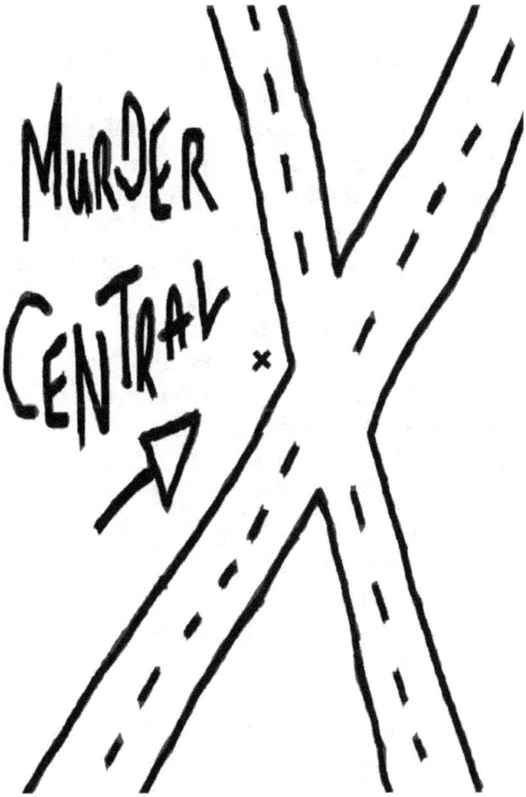
MURDER
CENTRAL

Stood around murder central for nearly an hour before I saw him bumping down the street. He was alone this time, gabbing on a cell phone and smoking a cigarette.

Hey Diablo! Mr. Diablo! Got a minute.

What the fuck chew want? Wait, I remember you. You's that crazy fool called my boy Sidearm a nigger.

I sincerely apologize for that, and you can relay that to him for me. I'm not a racist. My wife is, but I assure you I'm not.

You's a real crazy mutherfucker coming back here. You really wants to get merked don't chew?

Yes, in fact, that's exactly what I want.

You wants to get merked?

Yes.

For reals?

For reals.

Find somebody else, pig.

I'm not a cop.

If you ain't a cop you's a coo-coo-doo, and I don't deal with coo-coo-doos.

I'll give you a thousand bucks.

Thousand bucks ain't worth no 25 to life.

Two thousand.

Why you wants to get merked for?

It doesn't matter.

Matters to me.

Can you help me or not?

Ten grand.

I don't have ten grand.

Then you don't gots my services.

I can give you five.

Fi'? Let me ponder it.

It's an easy five grand. What's there to ponder?

Whether or not I trust you.

You can trust me.

Lift up yo shirt.

I'm not wired. Look. See. No wire. Trust me, you won't get caught. I promise.

Dead men can't keep promises.

It'll just be another random, senseless murder.

Cops already saw me wit chew. Cops know me.

The cops think I'm a drug addict. They won't give a shit.

You's a pushy mutherfucker.

Sorry. It's just...

Look, let me talk to some of my boyz, maybe I can outsource this project.

Great. Thanks.

Meet me here tomorrow at midnight and I'll let you know what's up.

Midnight. Got it. Perfect. Thanks.

You is really a coo-coo-doo, you know that. Never heard of nobody wanting to get themselves murked.

To each their own, right? I don't understand why people would be vegan, or heroin addicts, or be on a gluten free diet, but they do it.

What the fuck is gluten?

A protein composite found in foods processed from wheat.

Why people don't wanna eat it?

That's my point, Mr. Diablo. You'll just never understand why people do the things they do.

Tarkington came back to work today.

Lucky for him 'cause I'm going to get murdered any day now and if I'm dead there'll be no one to look after the bakery and make shit, blood, and human flesh muffins.

Must say though, being here with him when his jaw is wired isn't all the bad. Made me wonder how much better the world would be if no one could talk. You'd never get your feelings hurt, you'd never regret hurting someone else's feelings. If we all had our jaws wired we couldn't bite ourselves and spit the flesh into muffin batter. We couldn't ride the bus and shout/talk into cell phones and annoy the people sitting around us. Personally, I don't like the smell of tobacco smoke, but I'd rather smell tobacco than the emissions from the five million automobiles in this city. And I'd rather smell tobacco in a restaurant while eating than listen to some fermenting tampon at the table next to me talk to her condom boyfriend about what she should order. I'd rather see no cell phone signs posted everywhere than no smoking signs. Yeah, smoke is harmful to our health, but cell phones are harmful to our mental health. Used to be I'd see people waiting for the bus reading books or newspapers. Now, every tampon and condom is jerking around on their phones with a dazed zombie look on their faces ~ tap, tap, touching, punching buttons.

Sometimes I'll get curious.

Sometimes I'll peek over their shoulders to see what they're actually doing.

You know what they're doing sometimes.

Nothing.

They are tap, tap, touching, punching buttons, but the screen is ☐

Went to meet Diablo last night at the liquor store.

He brought the friend that's going to murder me.

He seemed like a pretty nice guy.

He had a teardrop tattoo under his left eye.

His name was Don't-worry-about-what-my-fucking-name-is.

Well, my name's Ernie.

I don't wanna know your fucking name. I just wants the green.

I don't have it on me.

Yo Diablo, I thought you says this joker's legit.

I am legit. I was under the assumption that this was just going to be a...powwow.

Is you's an Indian? Do I looks like I's an Indian?

No.

I should merk you for being ignorant.

For free?

Relax, dawg. He gots the digits. Don't you, Whitey?

For sure, I can bring it tomorrow.

Fi' grand.

Five thousand. Okay, deal. However, I do have some conditions.

Milky's got conditions. Okay Milky, let's hear these conditions.

It has to be done with a gun. I want a full clip fired into me so there's no chance I'll survive.

That's gonna be a problem.

How so?

As soon as shots get fired the black and white that patrols around here is gonna call it in, and there's gonna be a hundred cops swarming.

So what do you propose?

What do I propose? I love the way you talks, Milky. Like you's some college professor or sumpin. I propose I blow your fucking head off with a sawed-off shoty.

That'll work.

Gottamned right it'll work.

Can you rob me too?

*That'll cost extra.

How much?

For you, a thousand bucks.

Fine. But please don't do anything stupid with my stuff like pawn it. If I were you I'd toss it, otherwise, it might come back to you.

Does I looks stupid, Whitey? You may be a college professor but I gots street smarts.

I just want to make sure that nothing goes wrong.

Let me worry about that.

Whys you doin' this for anyway, Milky?

If you really must know Mr. Diablo, it's for my family.

You's gettin' murked for your family.

Yes.

You really is crazy.

So when's this going to happen?

Up to you, Snowflake.

How about Sunday?

That works for me.

Touching buttons.

The homosexual leech came home crying this morning because his homosexual condom boyfriend is going to rehab to overcome his technology addiction.

That's ridiculous.

It's a real disease, Mom.

Cancer is a real disease.

It's like a drug to him. He can't go five minutes without using his iPhone. It's totally affecting our relationship. He even got fired from the bar because of it.

Good. I hate it when I see people using phones at their jobs. Those Filipino cunts were constantly fucking around on their phones.

You're being very unsympathetic.

So now I gotta feel sorry for everybody with a problem? Does Paul feel sympathetic about me being indicted for murder?

I didn't tell him.

Why not?

Because I don't want him to know you've been accused of smothering an old lady in her sleep.

Maybe I have an addiction, like Paul. Yeah, maybe if I tell the judge I have a smothering old people addiction he'll understand and send me to smothering-old-people-rehab instead of prison.

Now you're being ridiculous, Mom. Technology addiction is like smoking. But instead of an oral fixation, it's a finger fixation.

Button touching addiction. What's next? Shit eating addiction.

What do you think, Dad?

I'm glad I'm getting murdered.

Everybody's different. I just hope Paul gets better.

That's sweet, Dad. I'll tell him you said that.
I'll whip him up a batch of chocolate chip.
Gluten free?
Is there any other kind?

Day 19, 844

THINGS TO DO
- go to bank
- make Paul shit cookies

- get murdered

Went to the bank.

Made Paul shit cookies.

Now I'm all dressed up in my funeral suit carrying a plastic shopping bag full of hundred dollar bill bricks.

Now I'm standing in front of the liquor store waiting for Don't-worry-about-what-my-fucking-name-is to blow my head off with a shotgun and rob me. Or rob me and then blow my head off with a shotgun.

It's past midnight.

The street is empty ~ except for my murderer.

He's walking briskly. His head is shifting left to right, right to left, scanning the street for witnesses.

There are no witnesses.

He whistles and beckons me over to the mouth of an alley across the street.

I obey like a dog.

Gimmie yo shit.

My shit?

Yo shit, gimmie it.

You mean my stuff.

Yeah!

I take off my necklace, my ring, my watch, my cufflinks.

The money!

You can take the money after.

Gimmie the money!

After!

Yo, I ain't clownin' Snowflake!

Where's your gun?

Gimmie the money!

You don't have a gun do you?

He grabs the plastic shopping bag.

I don't let go.

It's a tug-of-war.

He's pulling and I'm not letting go. He's shouting at me to give it up, and I'm screaming at him to kill me, just fucking kill me, it's not that hard.

The bag stretches to its breaking point and snaps, money bricks fling into the air.

Don't-worry-about-what-my-fucking-name-is grabs as many bundles as he can and runs off into the night leaving me still alive. Still suffering.

Suffering from this disease.

Consciousness.

Day 19, 846

The cock sucking leech.

The cock sucking leech comes home today crying again.

Paul's sick. Really sick.

Technology withdrawal?

Diphtheria.

How could that happen?

I don't know.

Maybe he has a shit eating addiction now.

Fuck you, Mom!

Hey, don't talk to your mother like that.

Ever since she's been indicted she's been acting like a bitch.

You'd be acting like a bitch too if you were framed by a bunch of Filipino whores and being accused of murdering a helpless old lady.

Not if I were guilty!

You little faggot!

Hey, hey, hey. Relax. Relax.

Now you're racist and prejudice.

Ernie, you'd better get this little fudge-packer away from me before I go off.

Come on, son. Let's have a chat in the kitchen, leave your mother alone. She's got a lot on her plate.

At least you care, Dad. You always have. I'm so tired of dealing with her. Her moods go up and down like an elevator.

It's a struggle for me too sometimes.

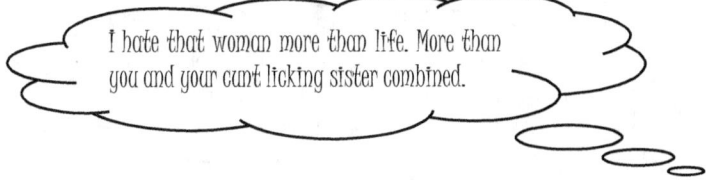

I hate that woman more than life. More than you and your cunt licking sister combined.

Honestly Dad, you've been the gluten that's held us together all these years. If it weren't for you, Connie and I would've left years ago. How do you put up with it? Why do you put up with it?

I made a promise.

That's it! You made a promise.

Should I have abandoned you guys?

I would've abandoned HER.

I'd be lying if I said I've never thought about it.

So why didn't you?

* I made a promise.*

That's bullshit, and you know it. No one deals with this for all this time because they made a promise.

I have.

Just say it!

Okay, I didn't want you and your sister to grow up without me.

What you really mean is that you didn't want us to grow up with only her around because we would've ended up as dingy as she is.

No, that's not what I mean.

Just admit it, Dad. Say it out loud for once. She's a fucking nut job. A crazy fucking bitch!

Hey, she's your mother.

Why can't you say it?

That's not how I feel.

Bullshit!

You're just upset right now.

Don't I have a right to be.

You have the right to feel however you want.

But I don't care how you feel. It burns my eyes to even look at you. I've loathed you since the day you came farting out of her putrid purple cunt.

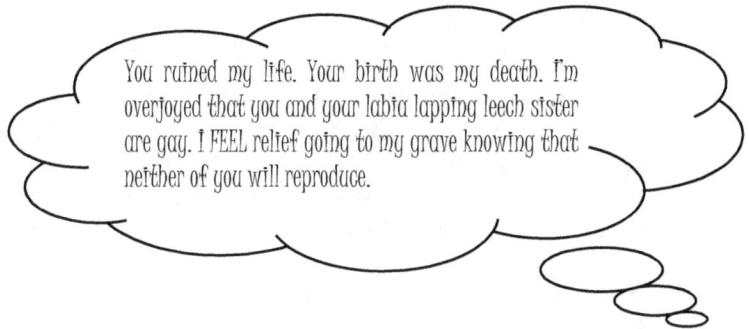

Why did she have children if she doesn't want to be a mother?

We grew up in a different time. The framework and blueprint still exists, but they're only recommendations now. When we grew up you were expected to get married, have 2.5 children, and work at a job, like it or not, until you retired or died.

That's retarded.

Well, that's what parents did, and that's what you were expected to do. Believe it or not, you and your sister are lucky to be alive in this time and place. Back in my day, you wouldn't be bringing Paul around to meet your parents. You wouldn't stand up in the Olive Garden and announce to the world that you're gay. Count your blessings.

I do, Dad. I do feel blessed. I'm blessed to have you. No, no, really. I really am. You're a special man. You never complain or whine about anything. I wish I was more like you, but unfortunately, I think I take after Mom. And that scares me.

Why?

She did it, Dad. You know she did it.

Yeah, I know she did it.

She's going away for the rest of her life, and I pray that nothing happens to you. Connie and I will be lost without you, Dad. Lost. Totally lost.

Don't worry, I'm not going anywhere.

Thanks for listening, Dad.

That's what I'm here for.
Who do you talk to?
*I talk to you, Connie, your mom."
*I mean who do you *really* talk to? Marriage, kids, it's all about venting, coming home after work and excreting, taking a mental shit. Getting it all out so it doesn't drive you crazy, so you don't shit on people. You never excrete, Dad. I've never heard you shit to Mom. You keep it all inside. You're mentally constipated.*
I get it out.
How?
I've always kept journals.
Really?
Yeah.
And writing helps?

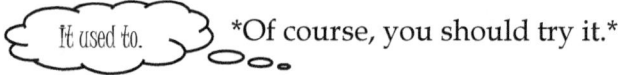 *Of course, you should try it.*

Maybe I will. Then I won't have to rely on Paul so much. Oh, by the way, can I borrow your iPhone? I snuck mine into the rehab to give to him. He was like, having a total meltdown.
Sure. Take it.
You're the best. Love you, Dad.
Love you too, son.

Tobacco.

Chewing tobacco.

Went by Clarence's to pick up some peppermint Skoal and he was bragging again that he's never been robbed.

Liquor store been robbed, pawn shop been robbed, damned fools even robbed the post office. But I ain't never been robbed.

Aren't you worried about the law of averages, Clarence?

What law of averages?

Well, if everyone around you has been robbed, the law of averages says that you're eventually going to get robbed.

Naw-uh, no sir. Not me. Never. No way.

Day 19, 853

Called the wrong number.
        Called the wrong number on purpose.
        *Oh my God, Ernie! It's so good to hear from you.
Wait, are you calling me or your life insurance company?*
        You.
        Really.
        Yeah.
        Why?
        I was wondering if you could help me out.
        Sure. What's up?
        I want to be murdered. And I want you to do it.
        I'd love to help out Ernie, but I'm a vegetarian.
        Oh yeah, that's right. I forgot.
        Sorry Ernie, I really wish I could help.
        It's okay.
        *Why do you want to die anyway? You have a better
life than me and I don't want to die. At least you have a
family, at least you're not ugly and lonely.*
        *I've never been honest with anybody, Vivian. But I'll
be honest with you right now. I don't like being alive. It's that
simple. I've tried to like it. I've done my best to like it. But I
don't. And I'm tired of trying. You think having a family
makes you feel companionship and fulfillment, but it only
makes me feel more isolated and discontent. I hate them
Vivian. I hate everyone. Humanity is a disease. I'm a disease.
Consciousness is a disease. And I've found the cure. Death.*
        So why don't you just kill yourself?
        *Then everyone will know. They'll all know I
was...unhappy. And I don't want them to know. I don't want
to be remembered like that. I've been wearing this mask for
fifty-four years and I'm not about to take it off now. Not when
I'm this close.*
        *Well, good luck with everything, Ernie. I hope you
find the relief, or peace, or whatever it is you're looking for.*
        The cure for consciousness.

Hero Dies in Hospital

Ernie Lobe, 54, husband and father of two, was fatally shot last night during a robbery attempt at The *Tobacco Hut* on the corner of Cherry Lane and Main Street South. According to the owner Clarence King, 67, two males rushed the booth with handguns and demanded money. Lobe, professional baker, attempted to stop the gunmen by grabbing their weapons. "They didn't shoot right away," said King. "They warned him to back off, but Ernie didn't listen. He tried to take them down. That's when the one guy shot. Then the other guy shot. Then they both started shooting. They must've shot him ten times. I never saw nothing like it, he was like Superman or something. He just kept going for them."

As of now the police have no other leads than the description King has given. One Hispanic male, early twenties, 5' 9'' 190 lbs with a tattoo on his neck. The other, a black male, mid-twenties, 5' 8'' to 5' 10'' approximately 170 lbs wearing a red hooded sweatshirt.

"Ernie wasn't just a customer," added King. "He was my friend. He'd been coming to my shop regularly for over thirty years. If it weren't for him I could be dead, or even worse, robbed. He was a hero. He stopped that robbery."

Lobe died from gunshot wounds on his way to the emergency room. He is survived by his son Charles, daughter Connie, and Brenda, his wife of thirty three years, who is currently on trial for the murder of 91 year old Agnes Cornworth.

Acknowledgements

My first thank you must go to Mom and Dad for still loving me even after all of the shit they've put up with from me over the years. My second thank you is to the tobacco and pharmaceutical companies for providing me and the world with an endless supply of cancer and psychotropic drugs.

About the Author

For the last six years Peter Jelen has been living, working, and travelling throughout Asia. He currently resides in Gimhae, South Korea. Check him out on www.peterjelen.com

Better Than God
Peter Jelen

ONLY HUMANS CAN BE HUMANE

Euthanasia is a firing squad, the Catholic Church brings the Son of Man back to life with the Shroud of Turin, doctors create imaginary mental disorders to further their careers, and God hands in his letter of resignation in the form of a suicide note while lonely young girls seek out pedophiles on the Internet just for some attention. Better Than God is a collection of dark and humorous fast-paced imaginative stories filled with unforgettable characters only Peter Jelen can provide.

$12.99
ISBN 13: 978-0988075016
192 Pages
BIASC: Short Stories

Better Than God

NOW:

I'M KISSING HIM goodbye for the last time. Tears are welling in my eyes. He doesn't know why I'm crying. He doesn't know he's at the airport. He doesn't know I've taped three hundred tablets of ecstasy to the inside of his thigh, and he's about to get on a one-way non-stop flight.

Of course, I've told him all of this many, many times, but he doesn't remember any of it.

He has Alzheimer's. And I promised I would kill him.

$^#*$)#&#(%&%&#(#(#)#%&%&%

Before:

One afternoon, a few months after he was diagnosed my mother phoned me at work completely frantic. My father was trying to leave the house naked, insisting he had to go to the city hall and file their marriage license.

By the time I got there he was gone, and she was sitting on the porch, her hands shaking, speaking to herself, a massive shiner under her eye from trying to stop him. A few hours later the police delivered him home without much sympathy. They'd found him waiting for the B-Line on Thurston Street standing in the bus shelter right next to Fairland Elementary School.

He was wrapped in a gray fireproof blanket, embarrassed and lucid. He hobbled upstairs to bed while me and my mother apologized and thanked the police. They saw the bruise on her face and warned us that things would only get worse.

"Consider getting full-time homecare," said one of the cops, "or put him in an assisted living facility. This can't happen again."

$^#*$)#&#(%&%&#(#(#)#%&%&%

So we hired a private nurse, a big Turkish guy from Ankara named Mustafa. We couldn't afford him full-time so he came late in the mornings and left in the early afternoon, that way my mom would only have to look after my father for a short time until I could get there after work. Mustafa was a podiatrist in Turkey, yet he never seemed embittered by the unfortunate fact that our government didn't consider him qualified enough to help feet that belonged to people standing on this part of the planet.

Mustafa was a liberal Muslim, and my father was a loose Orthodox. At the beginning, whenever my father was lucid they would talk about God together, and Mustafa would tell him about what the Koran says about Allah, and my father would tell Mustafa what the Gospels say about Jesus.

Mustafa was very gentle with my father, and he was good at controlling him whenever the disease took over and my father tried to leave the house, or insisted on doing something nonsensical. Sometimes he had to subdue him; literally hold the old man down on the floor and not let him up until the fit passed. Often times, when I would get there after work Mustafa would still be at the house looking after him, he'd have tears in his eyes, telling me that my father keeps begging to die, begging to be killed.

$^#*$)#&#(%&%&#(#(#)#%&%&%

Before long:

The lapses of lucidity were coming more frequently and with greater potency, sometimes lasting several hours, sometimes several days. And during every increasingly rare moment of clarity my father begged to die. Whoever was near he would grab by the hand, look deeply and clearly into their eyes, and with a hoarse whisper, he would say, "Kill me. Please, kill me."

Eventually Mustafa couldn't take it anymore. He came to me nearly six months after I'd hired him, asked me out on to the porch, sat me down and told me he was sorry.

"I'm not right for this," he said. "I work with feet."

"What can I do?"

"He's getting much worse, and I just can't...I'm having trouble watching it."

"So am I."

"He begs me to kill him, Michael."

"I know."

"I can't look into his eyes anymore."

"It's not easy for me, either. He's my father and I gotta watch this happen to him. I gotta wipe his ass and bathe him and feed him like he's another son. I don't even sleep anymore. I don't see my wife, my little boy."

"Put him in a home, Michael."

"I can't afford it. I can hardly afford you."

"Please, find someone else."

He finally sat next to me, prayed his hands together and then covered his face, washed it with dry hands.

"I'm thinking about going to the Netherlands," I said.

"They won't do it," he said. "It's too late. He's unfit to make the decision."

"But if he's lucid when they test him..."

"He's never lucid for more than a minute anymore, Michael."

"I'm going to have the doctor change his medication, if it works, I'm bringing him."

"And what about your mother?"

"I'm not going to tell her."

"But you'll tell me."

"You've been with him, Mustafa. You've see that look in his eyes when he begs. You know he wants this. And I don't know about you, but if it were me, if I ever get like that, I would want the same."

Mustafa nodded agreeably.

"You're a doctor, Mustafa. I know it's your oath to save people's lives, and I know your religion forbids this, but..."

"You want my opinion?"

"Yes."

"As a doctor, a Muslim, or a man?"

"As a man."

"He's lucid when he begs. He knows what he's become. Those flickers of awareness are making him suffer."

"Thank you."

Mustafa extended his hand and I took it, pulled him up from his seat and hugged him.

"Good-bye, my friend," he said. "And when he's there, tell him goodbye from me."

"I will."

$^#*$)#&#(%&%&#(#(#)#%&%&%

But it was impossible not to tell my mother. I had to let her say goodbye. I'd always thought it was unfair of God not to let us say goodbye to our loved ones. Instead he steals them from us in the middle of the night while they're asleep, or crushes them to death by a drunk driver, drowns them in a hurricane, or swallows them up with a tsunami, then he makes us weep and wail and say goodbye to a pile of useless flesh, bones, fingernails, and hair. Or even worse: a memory.

Now, here was my chance to do something better than God.

Here I called my mother into the kitchen, sat her down and let her know right away that I'd arranged a trip to the Netherlands, and that Dad wasn't coming back.

"But he's been getting better lately," she said.

"He's not getting better, Mom. It's the medication. He's not going to get better. You know he wants this, Mom."

"But your father's not God."

"And God's not him. God's not us. People can be humane, God can't. To hold onto Dad like this is our own selfishness. We're making him suffer."

"But at night, when he sleeps, when he's next to me, it's like it's always been, I need him there at night with me."

She tried to fight her tears but it was useless. I wrapped my arms around her bony shoulders and cried with her. For our suffering.

$^#*$)#&#(%&%&#(#(#)#%&%&%

Mustafa was right. It was too late, and the trip to Europe was all for nothing. The doctor I met couldn't assist him. He understood my predicament, my father's wishes, but my father didn't show a glimmer of awareness the entire consultation, and quite simply, he couldn't do it. I asked him if there were other options, other doctors that could help.

"Probably," he said, "but I can't recommend any for you."

$^#*$)#&#(%&%&#(#(#)#%&%&%

I took my father back to our hotel room and put him to bed. He slept peacefully. He slept and I wished he wouldn't wake up. He wasn't my father anymore. He wasn't even a human being anymore. He was a deformity. A shell. Empty. All of the memories he'd collected gone. Burned up like a photo album in a house fire. I wanted to take my pillow and cover his face, hold it there until he ceased breathing.

But I couldn't suffocate him.

I couldn't kill my father.

I didn't have the heart for that, even if I wouldn't get caught.

$^#*$)#&#(%&%&#(#(#)#%&%&%

The next morning I was in the lobby reading the news on the Internet, more specifically a report about an un-medicated schizophrenic British national that tried smuggling a kilo of cocaine into Beijing, was caught at customs, and sentenced to die by the end of the week. The article mentioned that the Chinese had no sympathy for the fact that the man was being used as a drug-mule with no idea about what was in his suitcase, or even aware of what he was doing.

That article sent me into the streets of Amsterdam asking shady looking people standing on street corners for ecstasy. It took me four days, but I gathered nearly 300 tablets.

Then I bought him a flight ticket to Beijing, put the ecstasy tablets in a balloon and taped it to the inside of my father's leg, and brought him to the airport.

$^#*$)#&#(%&%&#(#(#)#%&%&%

Now:

I'm kissing him goodbye for the last time. Tears are welling in my eyes. He doesn't know why I'm crying. He doesn't know he's at the airport. He doesn't know I will alert the authorities before the plane touches the ground. He doesn't know he'll be executed by the end of the week.

www.barebackpress.com
Hamilton, Ontario
Canada